He Who Wears the Glove Shall Rule!

"The Prophets of the Dark Side have foretold that the next Emperor shall wear the glove of Darth Vader," said an Imperial grand admiral, challenging Trioculus.

"And they know our destiny!" added a member of the Imperial Royal Guard.

Only *I* know the destiny of the Empire," thundered Trioculus, who didn't wear a glove on either hand. "And only *I* have the power of my father—the lightning power of the Dark Side!"

Trioculus raised his arms and bolts of lightning shot from his fingertips. The lightning crackled in two directions, striking both the member of the Imperial Royal Guard and the grand admiral who dared to question him.

The shock from the lightning was too much for the warlords. The men fell to their knees, pleading with Trioculus to stop as they quaked and thrashed on the ground, moaning, while the electricity sizzled all around them.

THE GLOVE OF DARTH VADER

STAR WARS

The Adventure C

STAR WARS®

Book 1

THE GLOVE OF DARTH VADER

PAUL DAVIDS
AND HOLLACE DAVIDS

Pencils by Benton Jew,
Industrial Light & Magic
Finished Art by Karl Kesel

A BANTAM SKYLARK BOOK®
NEW YORK · TORONTO · LONDON · SYDNEY · AUCKLAND

RL 4, 008–012

THE GLOVE OF DARTH VADER
A Bantam Skylark Book/July 1992

Cover art by Drew Struzan
Interior pencils by Benton Jew, Industrial Light & Magic
Finished interior art by Karl Kesel

ISBN 0-553-15887-2

Published simultaneously in the United States and Canada

Bantam Books are published by Bantam Books, a division of Bantam Doubleday
Dell Publishing Group, Inc. Its trademark, consisting of the words "Bantam
Books" and the portrayal of a rooster, is Registered in U.S. Patent and Trademark
Office and in other countries. Marca Registrada. Bantam Books, 1540 Broadway,
New York, New York 10036.

PRINTED IN THE UNITED STATES OF AMERICA

OPM   19   18   17   16   15   14   13   12   11

To Jordan and Scott,
May the Force be with you . . .

Acknowledgments

With thanks to George Lucas, the creator of Star Wars, to Lucy Wilson for her devoted guidance, to Charles Kochman for his unfailing insight, and to West End Games for their wonderful Star Wars sourcebooks—also to Betsy Gould, Judy Gitenstein, Peter Miller, and Richard A. Rosen for their advice and help.

The Rebel Alliance

Luke Skywalker

Princess Leia

Han Solo

Chewbacca

See-Threepio (C-3PO)

Artoo-Detoo (R2-D2)

Mon Mothma

Admiral Ackbar

The Empire

Trioculus

Grand Moff Hissa

Emdee-Five (MD-5)

Grand Moff Muzzer

Grand Moff Dunhausen

Grand Moff Thistleborn

Captain Dunwell

Aqualish Alien

A long time ago,
in a galaxy
far, far away...

The Adventure Continues . . .

It was an era of darkness, a time when the evil Empire ruled the galaxy. Fear and terror spread across every planet and moon.

Emperor Palpatine, the Imperial dictator, reigned, aided by his second-in-command, Darth Vader. Together they tried to crush all who resisted them—but still the Rebel Alliance survived.

The Rebel Alliance was formed by heroic men, women, and aliens, united against the Empire in their valiant fight to restore freedom and justice to the galaxy.

Luke Skywalker joined the Rebels after his uncle purchased a pair of droids known as See-Threepio (C-3PO) and Artoo-Detoo (R2-D2). The droids were on a mission to save the beautiful Princess Leia. Leia was a Rebel Alliance leader who was being held captive by the Empire, and was caught in the clutches of the evil Darth Vader.

In his quest to save Princess Leia, Luke was assisted by Han Solo, the dashing pilot of the spaceship *Millennium Falcon*, and Han's copilot, Chewbacca, a hairy alien known as a Wookiee.

Han and Luke eventually succeeded in rescuing the Rebel princess, but their struggle against the Empire did not end there. Luke and his ragtag group of Rebel freedom fighters battled armor-clad stormtroopers, and mile-long star destroyers, and faced the Empire's mightiest weapon of all—the Imperial Death Star. The Death Star was a battle station as big as a moon, with the power to destroy an entire planet. It was exploded by the Rebels in a deadly mission. The Empire soon built a second Death Star though, this one even larger and more powerful than the first.

In the course of his adventures Luke sought out the wise old hermit, Obi-Wan Kenobi, who became Luke's first teacher in the ways of the Jedi Knights.

The Jedi Knights, an ancient society of brave and noble warriors, were the protectors of the Old Republic in days before the Empire was formed. The Jedi believed that victory comes not just from physical strength but from a mysterious power called the Force.

The Force lies hidden deep within all things. It has two sides: one side that can be used for good, the other side a power of absolute evil.

In training to become a Jedi Knight, Obi-Wan Kenobi sent Luke to study under a great Jedi Master, Yoda. From Yoda, Luke discovered some startling truths about himself—Princess Leia was actually his twin sister and his father was none other than Darth Vader. Luke learned that Darth Vader had once been a Jedi Knight, but Vader was lured to the ways of the Dark Side by Emperor Palpatine and then became obsessed with power and consumed with hatred.

The Jedi Masters realized that it was Luke's destiny to battle his own father, or else the Dark Side would triumph. There were two confrontations between father and son, both of them duels fought with blazing lightsabers.

Before Darth Vader's death, Luke helped his father come to the understanding that Emperor Palpatine had turned him against everyone and everything he had ever loved. Darth Vader then destroyed the Emperor, hurling him down into the power core of the Death Star. Then the Death Star itself was destroyed, exploded in a Rebel attack.

With the Empire's evil leaders gone and their battle station destroyed, a new era has begun. Imperial warlords have been fighting for power among themselves, but no one knows who will seize control. However, the Prophets of the Dark Side have foretold that a new Emperor will soon arise, and on his hand he shall wear an indestructible symbol of evil—the glove of Darth Vader!

CHAPTER 1
Droids on a Mission

See-Threepio's frantic voice echoed through the Droid Repair Shop on Yavin Four, the fourth moon of the planet Yavin.

"But, Master Luke," Threepio was saying, "Kessel has always been *last* on my list of places in the galaxy I'd like to see. Particularly on a dangerous spy mission without my own head."

"You're only getting a different head *cover*, not a whole new head," Luke Skywalker said to his golden, human-shaped droid. He bent to examine a used droid head on a shelf. "We're not going to touch a single one of your microcircuits. We just don't want you to be noticed in a crowd of Kessel droids."

The Kessel droid head Luke was holding had a punched-in, evil-looking face. It was a face that didn't match Threepio's gentle personality at all. "What do you think of this one?" asked Luke.

"*That* one? There's something lacking in your taste, Master Luke. It's unsightly—and . . . and it's green!" Threepio stammered.

"Didn't I tell you about your new color-plating?"

"You're not going to make me green, are you?"

Threepio exclaimed, waving his arms.

"Don't panic," said Luke. "Your gold color will be restored, along with your usual head cover, when the mission is over. Come on, let's get started."

BZZZZZZZT!

Luke pressed his inter-office communications device, signaling the Droid Modification Team that Threepio was ready. The team was a group of Too-Onebee technical droids that specialized in repairing other droids and replacing their worn-out parts. The Too-Onebees brought with them Artoo-Detoo, a barrel-shaped droid that they had just finished modifying. Artoo now resembled a dark green Kessel mining droid, complete with a Kessel insignia on his dome.

"Dweeeet bchooo tzniiiiiiiit!" beeped Artoo-Detoo, turning his new dome left and right so that Luke and Threepio would notice.

"No, I don't think you look wonderful," replied Threepio, who was an expert at translating six million galactic languages and understood all of Artoo's beeps, buzzes, and whistles.

Walking away from his little friend, Threepio reluctantly left with the Droid Modification Team. He returned an hour later.

"I hope you're satisfied," Threepio said with dismay.

"You look perfect," Luke replied with a smile. "Come on, we have to get to the new Senate. You don't want to miss the beginning of Mon Mothma's briefing, do you?"

Luke walked toward the door quickly, thinking to himself how fortunate the Alliance was to have a distinguished and brilliant woman like Mon Mothma as its leader. "When Mon Mothma explained our strategy for the battle against the Death Star, you were on time to hear her then—and this is no time to be late, either, Threepio. Especially since all of the key members of SPIN will be there."

SPIN was short for the Senate's Planetary Intelligence Network, a secret organization within the Alliance's new galactic government.

WHOOOOSH!

Luke's airspeeder zoomed over the treetops of the rain forest on Yavin Four, dodging the peaks of the old pyramids. Soon he could see many of the elaborate structures that had been built by a long-vanished race. He saw the Great Temple. And to his left the Temple of the Blueleaf Cluster. And up ahead the Palace of the Woolamander, where the new Senate met.

It was nearly twilight when Luke landed the airspeeder. He hurried Threepio and Artoo up the ramp to the main Senate entrance and they proceeded down a stone hallway until they reached the briefing room.

Seated at the conference table were two human women, two human men, and two aliens. The women were Mon Mothma and Princess Leia; the men were

Han Solo and Lando Calrissian, the governor of Cloud City on the planet Bespin; and the aliens were Chewbacca, the Wookiee, and Admiral Ackbar, the sad-eyed fishman and war hero from the watery world of Calamari.

Luke took his place at the center of the table, with Threepio and Artoo standing nearby.

"Well, kid," Han said to Luke, "you sure did a great job on these droids. If I didn't know what was going on, I'd swear I was on Kessel."

"Thanks, Han. Coming from you, that really means a lot," Luke said to his friend.

"Kessel is a planet that all experienced cargo pilots try to avoid," said Han. "Especially me. But a few times, when there was a fortune to be made from transporting spice, I flew the trip from Kessel anyway, against my better judgment. In fact, I've made the Kessel Run in the *Millennium Falcon* in less than twelve standard timeparts."

"You told me that the day I first met you, back in the cantina at the Mos Eisley spaceport on Tatooine," said Luke. "Remember? When I showed up with Obi-Wan Kenobi and—"

"Yeah, I remember, kid, now that you mention it," interrupted Han. He knitted his brows and frowned. "Well, take my word for it—things have gotten even meaner on Kessel since then. And it's tough times there for spice traders and old Corellian space pirates like me. These days, if they even *suspect* you might be loyal to the Alliance, they send you straight to the spice mines—to be a slave for life!"

"Which brings us to the urgency of the Kessel mission," Mon Mothma said strongly. "Thousands of grand moffs, evil warlords, stormtroopers, Imperial droids, and enemy officers from the Empire are arriving at Kessendra Stadium on Kessel for a big gathering in their capital city."

She turned to Artoo-Detoo and continued. "Artoo, your data banks now contain information on every important Imperial who might be at that meeting, including all those who may have ambitions to become the new leader of the Empire. You also have data on the Prophets of the Dark Side. There seems to be much controversy about the latest prophecy of the Supreme Prophet of the Dark Side, Kadann."

Mon Mothma touched a button on the conference table console and a holo-projector flashed Kadann's words in midair:

> *After Palpatine's fiery death*
> *Another leader soon comes to command the Empire*
> *And on his right hand he does wear*
> *The glove of Darth Vader!*

A menacing silence fell over the briefing room.

"Ptooog bziiiini?" beeped Artoo, as his new dome rotated back and forth.

"He wants to know how the right-hand glove of Darth Vader can still exist," said Threepio.

"Unlike the left-hand glove, the right glove was

made to be indestructible," Mon Mothma replied. "A symbol of evil that would survive forever. After Luke cut off Darth Vader's right hand in their lightsaber duel, the glove was believed to have been hurled out into space when the Death Star exploded.

"According to our intelligence reports," she continued, "the glove has not yet been found. We have teams out searching for it, but it's possible that someone at the Kessel meeting might have found the glove already and claim to be the new Emperor."

Suddenly Mon Mothma's holo-projector created an image of a meteor. "Threepio and Artoo, this may look like a meteor, but it's actually your landing pod," she explained. "Admiral Ackbar and his fellow Calamarians built this especially for your mission."

"We guarantee that it will do the job," Admiral

Ackbar said confidently.

Lando smiled and nudged his friend Han Solo, who was sitting beside him. "Han has been kind enough to offer me a ride back to Bespin," said Lando, "so that I can get back to Cloud City for some urgent business. On our way, as we pass near Kessel, we'll eject the pod from the *Millennium Falcon,* right, Han?"

"Sure thing," Han put in.

"The pod should get through enemy defenses undetected," said Mon Mothma, turning to the droids. "It's also been designed for your escape from Kessel. When your mission is over and you reboard, the pod will shed its meteor coating so that it will look like a spherical Imperial probe droid. Then it will automatically soar to the upper atmosphere, where you'll be picked up by an Imperial command speeder we captured and modified with hyperdrive for interplanetary flight—Command Speeder 714-D."

Threepio rubbed the back of his new metal head cover. He thought he could hear a fuse popping somewhere inside his electronic brain. This was all so shocking! "And what if we get lost on Kessel?" he asked timidly.

"You droids managed to find Jabba the Hutt's palace on Tatooine all by yourselves," Luke reminded Threepio.

"And you even helped rescue Han when he was frozen in suspended animation inside a block of solid carbonite," said Leia.

"*Grrrowff!*" Chewbacca agreed.

"On the outside chance that you droids do get lost," Mon Mothma added, "remember that we've programmed Artoo-Detoo's data banks with maps of Kessel that we recovered from an escaped slave. Those maps show every street in the capital city of Kessendra and the layout of Kessendra Stadium—even the slaves' secret escape tunnel you'll be using to get into the stadium."

At last Mon Mothma concluded the briefing and sent everyone to get a good night's rest before the mission began.

"Master Luke, sir," said Threepio in a sinking voice. "Are you sure there's no one else in the Alliance better suited for this mission than Artoo-Detoo and me?"

"You computed the odds yourself, Threepio," replied Luke. "I asked you what the chances are of any human or alien who's loyal to the Alliance getting back from Kessel alive."

Threepio nodded. "Only one chance in twelve thousand six hundred," he said, sighing. "Very well, then. It's all for the best. We droids are replaceable, after all."

Under the starlit sky of Yavin Four, Han Solo walked Princess Leia to her quarters.

"Your highness," said Han. "After Chewie and I drop off the droids in the meteor pod on Kessel and take Lando back to Cloud City . . . well, I don't know exactly how to put this . . . I'm not planning on coming back for a while."

"But, Han," Princess Leia protested, "you know how important you are to SPIN."

"Maybe so, but Lando's offered me a lease on a piece of sky near Cloud City. I've always dreamed of having a place of my own, and I figure it's about time Chewie and I built my dream sky house."

"Can't you put it off until we know what's going on with the new Emperor?" asked Leia.

"Princess, there's always something important that seems to come up before I can take care of my own dreams. Time is running out. And a man's got to do what he's got to do."

"If that's the way you want it, Han," Leia said, not quite understanding him. She turned away.

"I'm going to miss you, Princess," said Han, taking her hand. "May the Force be with you."

CHAPTER 2
Lightning Power of the Dark Side

As the *Millennium Falcon* came out of hyperdrive and slowed below lightspeed, Han and Chewie deliberately navigated into the heart of a huge electrical storm in Kessel's outer atmosphere. The black lightning clouds were an unsuspecting place from which to eject the meteor pod.

ZHWEEEEEK! The cargo door screeched as it opened.

Soon the pod was dropping toward Kessel, buffeted by strong winds, its outer rock-coating struck by lightning, its interior heated by friction. But it kept adjusting its path of descent, taking the droids to where they needed to go.

The worst part for Threepio and Artoo was the landing. The meteor pod bounced into a rocky mountainside, rolled into a few bushy Kesselian trees, and finally came to a stop within an easy walk to the hidden entrance of the slaves' escape tunnel.

The pod's hatch door opened and the two disguised droids emerged to face the looming mountains set against an eerie pink sky. The electrical storm had ended.

"I'm certainly glad droids don't get dizzy, or I wouldn't be able to stand up for days," said Threepio. He glanced at their pod. "Look, Artoo, our meteor pod looks like just another boulder against the craggy terrain. It should be safe here until we return. That is, *if* we return."

They found the underground passageway, and Threepio pushed away the rocks that concealed the entrance. Soon they were heading into the tunnel, which had a faint luminous glow from the many spice-covered rocks.

In the semidarkness Threepio asked Artoo to project Mon Mothma's holographic map of the tunnel interior. "That's upside down!" Threepio exclaimed. "Honestly, you don't expect me to stand on

my head to read that map, do you?"

Artoo flipped his projection so that the map was right-side up. After studying it, Threepio plunged ahead. With every clattering step, he took Artoo closer and closer to Kessendra Stadium, which was at the very edge of the capital city of this Imperial slave planet.

"Hurry—this way, Artoo!" said Threepio. "Mon Mothma's map said the entrance to the stadium is somewhere down here!"

"*Dweep boooooweep*," beeped Artoo, rolling along as fast as he could.

"No, it isn't my fault that we're here," replied Threepio as he walked even faster. "We do have our orders, you know. Let's just hope that nobody finds out who we really are. Otherwise, they'll take us apart and use us for spare parts—or worse!"

Threepio continued talking without pause, since droids never have to stop to catch their breath the way organic creatures do. "It's positively horrifying. Half the Imperial officers in the galaxy are gathered together, practically right above our heads, and goodness knows what evil plans they're making."

Kessendra Stadium was the frequent site of gladiator games in which slaves fought to the death, while sportsmen from throughout the galaxy placed bets. Today, however, there would be no gladiator games.

"*Droot boopa zinnn*," beeped Artoo.

"I quite agree with you," replied Threepio, nodding his head. "I'd have thought they'd given up the war, too, when their second Death Star blew up, and when Emperor Palpatine and Darth Vader died, and—Oh no!"

Threepio walked into a metal column and clattered to the ground. "Now look what you made me do." He quickly picked himself up and checked his plating for dents. "You're always distracting me, Artoo!"

Artoo gave a singsong series of toots and whistles. *"Reewooo dweet? Beeeeza zooon?"*

"No, there aren't any droid-eating monsters down here. Now stop babbling and help me look for the entrance to the stadium and— Gracious! There it is back there! Why didn't you tell me we'd

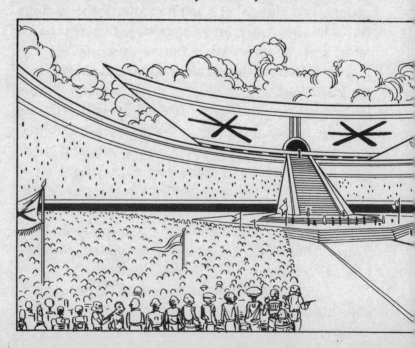

passed it, you nearsighted hunk of tin!"

"*Vrrrr BEEEEEP!*"

"Well, the same to you!"

Threepio cautiously opened the creaking metal door and sneaked out of the darkness, with Artoo rolling along behind him. The pink sky was so bright it nearly blinded Threepio's eye-sensors.

When his sensors cleared, Threepio could see that they were at the lower level of the stadium, where slaves and droids were gathered to listen to the speeches. All around them were green humanoid droids with menacing heads and barrel-shaped spice-mining droids, who looked just like Threepio and Artoo did in their disguises.

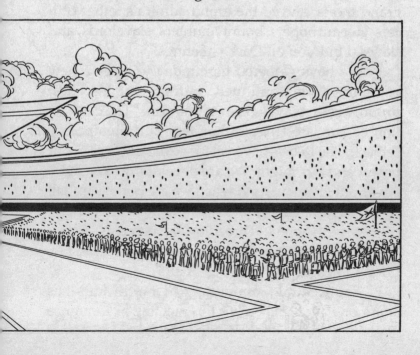

Above them, in the comfortable bleacher seats that surrounded the pit of slaves, were so many Imperial officers and stormtroopers that at first they all seemed to blur together. Artoo raised a long-distance sensor to get a close-up view. Then the barrel-shaped droid began matching the faces he saw with the faces and names of the Imperial officers in his data banks.

The crowd became quiet as a grand moff, one of the Empire's regional governors, began to speak. The beady-eyed grand moff was bald and his teeth had been filed into sharp, spearlike points.

"I am Grand Moff Hissa," he announced, just as Artoo figured out who he was. "And to my fellow grand moffs, and to the grand admirals, other officers, stormtroopers, bounty hunters, slavelords, and slaves, I bid you all Dark Greetings!

"We have gathered here today to mark a new beginning," he continued, puffing out his chest proudly to display his brown uniform. "The destruction of our latest Death Star was but a temporary setback. The Rebels have yet to see the full fury of our power and our might. We are developing even more advanced weapons, and when we are done, we shall rule the entire galaxy and *crush* the Rebel Alliance."

As he listened, Threepio whispered to Artoo. "Oh, dear, I certainly don't like the sound of this. No, I don't like the sound of this at all."

"The Central Committee of Grand Moffs has summoned you all here for this meeting to announce our new leader," said Grand Moff Hissa in a bellowing voice. "Even though Emperor Palpatine is dead, his line continues. For many years you have heard rumors that the Emperor had a son. But our departed Emperor and the Central Committee of Grand Moffs always denied those rumors, for reasons of Imperial security. However, today I am authorized to inform you that the Emperor *did* indeed have a son—a son who shall be our new chosen one!"

The stadium was filled with gasps of shock and surprise at this revelation.

"The Emperor's son has lived among you on Kessel for many years now, keeping his true identity a carefully guarded secret," Grand Moff Hissa continued. "And now at last the time has come for the Emperor's son to take his rightful place as heir to the Empire."

"Who is the Emperor's son?" shouted a grand admiral.

There was a suspenseful moment of silence.

Then a huge, black door suddenly opened, and a tall mutant dressed in black came out to face the gathering.

"Friends of the Empire," Grand Moff Hissa announced, "I present to you the son of Emperor Palpatine—Trioculus, the Supreme Slavelord of Kessel!"

But instead of cheering, a frightened hush crept through the crowd at the sight of the new ruler. Trioculus was known to be a ruthless and merciless slavelord, one who had sent many slaves to their deaths.

Threepio could see that Trioculus looked powerful and threatening. But he was surprised that he wasn't ugly like Darth Vader and Emperor Palpatine had been. In fact, Trioculus was almost handsome. Except for one thing—

Two of Trioculus's eyes were right where Threepio expected them to be, on either side of his nose. However, it was Trioculus's third eye, right in the middle of his forehead, that made him look rather unusual.

Threepio bent down to talk quietly to Artoo. "A mutant—part human, part alien," he said. "Quite surprising. I've certainly never heard any gossip that Emperor Palpatine had a son by a three-eyed alien woman. Have you?"

From Artoo's beeps and buzzes, Threepio quickly learned many things he had never known before. For instance, Artoo's data banks revealed that some old Imperial stormtroopers *did* believe that the Emperor had had a son with three eyes, a son who lived on Kessel. However, when the Rebel Alliance had investigated that story, no evidence had ever been found. Now, however, the Alliance would have to investigate the situation again.

Artoo's rapid beeps revealed more about Trioculus, information from Mon Mothma's secret Alliance files on the slavelords of the Kessel spice mines.

Trioculus had a reputation for being among the

most evil and cruel of the Kessel slavelords, personality traits that developed when Trioculus was just a child. As the only mutant in his school on Kessel, he was teased and hit constantly by the other students who made fun of his third eye. Trioculus became obsessed with fighting back and taking revenge. He became the schoolyard bully, and he learned how to make his classmates fear him, by spying on them and reporting those who didn't follow the rules.

As Trioculus grew older, he studied the history of warfare and Imperial military tactics. That was when he had first become devoted to gaining total control over both his enemies and his friends.

Trioculus had few friends. But it was the quality of his allies that counted, not the quantity. Through his study of warfare he had won friends among important Imperial officers—especially the spike-toothed Grand Moff Hissa, who respected Trioculus's total loyalty to the Imperial cause.

And so, as one of Grand Moff Hissa's pets, Trioculus had come up from the ranks of overseers of the spice mines. Soon afterward, again with Grand Moff Hissa's help, Trioculus had been appointed Lord Overseer and Supreme Slavelord.

The crowd continued to watch in hushed silence, as Trioculus began to speak in a cold, throaty voice. "My father, the Emperor, had many powers of the Dark Side. But without three eyes he could never achieve perfection. It was known by the ancients that a Dark Lord with three eyes has a secret strength possessed by none other. And so it is my destiny to rule over my father's Empire and bring us the glory that he never achieved!"

Grand Moff Hissa came forward. "We have heard from Trioculus, the Emperor's son, and we shall obey him, one and all! Prepare to bow and accept your new Emperor!"

A member of the Imperial Royal Guard stood up and shouted out a troublesome question in a booming voice.

"Just a moment, Grand Moff Hissa!" said the bold and foolhardy Royal Guard member. "Lord Trioculus, are you aware that there are others who claim to be the new ruler of the Empire? I have been to the planet Gargon. There, Grand Admiral Grunger says *he* is our new leader. And *he* has a fleet of thirty star destroyers!"

"I shall deal with him when I am ready," Trioculus said. "He will learn who is the rightful Emperor!"

Then an admiral stood to speak. "How can you claim to be the new chosen one when you do not wear Darth Vader's glove? The Prophets of the Dark Side have said that the next Emperor shall wear—"

"As the Emperor's son," shouted Trioculus, "it is through my blood that I rule, not with some glove!"

"But the Prophets of the Dark Side are powerful!" declared the member of the Imperial Royal Guard. "They foretold that the Rebels would blow up both Death Stars—and they even knew *when* they would be destroyed. They saw the future. Therefore they must know our destiny!"

"Only *I* know the destiny of the Empire," thundered Trioculus, "and only *I* have the power of my father and more—including the lightning power of the Dark Side!"

Trioculus raised his arms and bolts of lightning shot from his fingertips. The lightning crackled in two directions, striking both the member of the Imperial Royal Guard and the grand admiral who dared to question him.

The men fell to their knees, pleading with Trioculus to stop as they quaked and thrashed on the ground, moaning, while the electricity sizzled all around them.

At last Trioculus showed mercy on them and lowered his hands. "Now who will be the first officer to step forward and pledge his loyalty to me?" he demanded.

"I will!" shouted a general.

"No, let it be me!" shouted a grand moff. He rushed forward to be the first to bow down before Trioculus, and Trioculus accepted him.

After Trioculus listened to the officers pledge their vows of loyalty, he raised his arms, turned his back, and left through the huge black door. Grand Moff Hissa followed him.

Throughout the stadium everyone was talking about what they had just seen.

"I think we'd better get out of here, Artoo."

Threepio turned to look for the little droid. "Hey, wait for me!" he said, noticing that Artoo was already heading back toward the entrance to the underground passageway.

Threepio hurried to catch up with Artoo. As they approached the door to the tunnel, they saw that it was surrounded by stormtroopers—and the stormtroopers were bolting it shut!

CHAPTER 3
The Seven Words of Trioculus

Trioculus, surrounded by stormtrooper bodyguards, departed from Kessendra Stadium with Grand Moff Hissa. He was also accompanied by Emdee-Five (MD-5), his droid with a narrow head and shining eyes.

They rode in an armored landspeeder limousine to the large, black metal palace where Trioculus had lived since his promotion to Lord Overseer and Supreme Slavelord of the Spice Mines.

Upon their arrival Emdee went directly to the huge kitchen to warn Trioculus's chef to complete the preparations for the celebration banquet.

Soon Trioculus and Grand Moff Hissa were joined by a small, select group of grand moffs loyal to Trioculus and a grand admiral from the planet Gargon. Together they sat at a very long banquet table while a servant brought in trays filled with Whaladon meat, a delicacy that was reserved only for the Imperial ruling class and forbidden to stormtroopers and slaves. Whaladon meat was especially prized because it was thought to be a source of strength.

Whaladons were huge whale-like creatures, mammals that lived only in the oceans of the watery planet Calamari. They were highly intelligent and wise, and it was against the laws of Calamari to kill them. Still, a huge, illegal Whaladon hunting operation existed in Calamari's waters. In fact, even though Whaladons were an endangered species, there were more Whaladon hunters on Calamari than ever before, led by Captain Dunwell, a trusted friend of the Central Committee of Grand Moffs.

After Trioculus and his guests finished their dinner and while dessert was being served, Grand Moff Hissa announced that the new Emperor had something important to tell them. The guests became silent as Trioculus, who was in the place of honor at the head of the table, stood and drew himself up to his full, towering height.

He spoke seven words.

"Find me the glove of Darth Vader!" he said in a

booming voice. Then he stared at them with his third eye, causing his loyal officers to shudder.

Grand Moff Hissa understood the difficult task before them. The Central Committee of Grand Moffs had declared Trioculus to be the new Emperor. But if someone else found the glove and wore it, then Kadann, the Supreme Prophet of the Dark Side, might declare that Trioculus was not the rightful heir to the throne and should be deposed.

If that happened, the Central Committee of Grand Moffs would lose their credibility and would probably also lose their influence and power in running the Empire. Grand Moff Hissa was determined, at any cost, not to let that happen. In fact, all friends and allies of the Central Committee of Grand Moffs were being notified immediately that if any of them found the glove, he or she should notify Trioculus and turn it over to him at once.

To the other grand moffs, Hissa said: "We have heard our leader's words, and we shall do as he says. From each of your planets you will send out probe droids to search for the glove of Darth Vader. I shall send probes to search the forest moon of Endor and the space that surrounds it, scanning the area where the Death Star exploded."

Grand Moff Muzzer, who was the plumpest and most round-faced of the grand moffs, spoke his mind. "Space is vast and the glove very small. Perhaps you expect too much of the Empire's probe droids."

"Probe droids can find a bomb that's no bigger

than a man's hand," replied Grand Moff Hissa, "so they should have no trouble finding a glove. Especially one that is indestructible."

"We will need a new, secret home base," said Trioculus, turning his attention to another matter of business. "I have yet to decide where. I will now hear your suggestions."

Several of the grand moffs squirmed in their seats. This was new to them, entirely new. Emperor Palpatine had never asked them for suggestions.

A few moments passed before one of the grand moffs grew bold enough to speak. "I suggest the planet Tatooine," said Grand Moff Dunhausen, who wore earrings, little ornaments shaped like laser pistols. "We can take over the Mos Eisley spaceport!"

Trioculus dismissed the idea immediately. "That useless planet where Jabba the Hutt died? Do you think I want the Empire to waste its time eliminating sand people like the Tusken Raiders and those two-bit traders, the jawas?"

There was a longer silence before the next suggestion came. "Bespin!" said Grand Moff Thistleborn, whose bushy eyebrows touched each other in the middle and curled up at the ends. "Let's take over Cloud City!"

Trioculus sneered. "We already have a barge full of factories for building weapons and mining tibanna gas on Bespin. Besides, Cloud City isn't a fit place to train our troops."

"Dagobah?" offered the grand admiral from Gargon.

"You're wasting my time!" Trioculus shouted, slamming his fist down on the table. The dishes rattled and a serving flask of zoochberry cream fell on its side.

"Hoth?" Grand Moff Hissa said hesitantly.

Trioculus's scowl changed to a sly smile. "Very good, Grand Moff Hissa," he said. "You suggest the coldest, most miserable of all the frozen ice planets. Give me your reasoning."

"The new base should be located on a world that the Rebel Alliance wouldn't consider important," Grand Moff Hissa began. "Preferably a world where Imperial stormtroopers won't be too comfortable— comfortable men grow lazy and rebellious. There are still bases and military bunkers on Hoth that the Rebels once used before our four-legged AT-AT walk-ers chased them off the planet," he continued. "All we have to do is move in!"

Trioculus gave the order.

All loyal warlords would transport their Impe-rial military equipment to Hoth—the strike cruisers, frigates, and shuttles; the star galleons and star de-stroyers; the torpedo spheres and mobile command bases; the four-legged AT-AT snow-walkers, probe droids, and hoverscouts. Everything!

The grand admiral from Gargon suddenly rose to his feet. "You can't do this, Trioculus!" he shouted. "You're being too hasty. Until you find the glove of

Darth Vader, you won't be accepted as the new Emperor. What if Grand Admiral Grunger finds it first and—"

ZING!

The grand admiral fell forward onto the banquet table and spoke no more.

The grand moffs looked from one to the other with raised eyebrows. Most of them had expected the lightning power from Trioculus's fingertips to kill the grand admiral. But it wasn't Trioculus's style to exert himself to execute just anyone. He had instructed Grand Moff Hissa to take care of that kind of dirty work, especially in the case of a traitor interfering with a high-level Imperial conference.

And so the deed was done by Hissa with one short blast from his sidearm laser pistol.

Threepio and Artoo were lost on the streets of Kessendra. Unable to exit the stadium the same way they had entered it, they quickly joined the flow of droids streaming away from the event, hoping they wouldn't be noticed. Walking around the city, they hadn't found one street sign that matched the information in Artoo's data banks.

"Tzoooooot gniiiiiizba!" Artoo beeped in frustration.

"Calm down, Artoo, there must be some mistake," said Threepio. "We'll find our way."

"Chpeeeeeeez phoooooch!" tooted Artoo.

"Then let's go down to the next street and check that one," replied Threepio, heading south.

"*Pchoook ftiiiiz mebiiiiing kniiiiish!*" Artoo beeped noisily when they came to the next sign.

Threepio shook his head in dismay. "Slavelord Boulevard. No, this definitely isn't Spice Mines Avenue. It seems that all these streets have been renamed since Mon Mothma got that data."

The two droids wandered along the twisting streets of the city. The boulevards were bustling with stormtroopers and spice transport vehicles went bouncing past. As Threepio and Artoo crossed an avenue, they were almost run over by some Imperial officers who were riding in a landspeeder limousine.

After hours of going around in circles, Threepio and Artoo finally made their way out of the capital city to the very edge of the mountains that were filled with spice mines.

"I wasn't cut out to be a spy," Threepio declared as he finally located a path through the Kesselian trees. "I should go back to working with binary load lifters. That was my first job. I'm still not sure why I left."

"*Deeeeewooop broooop!*" tooted Artoo. A tiny radar screen popped out of the little droid's head and began swiftly spinning around.

"I certainly *hope* we get back to Yavin Four," replied Threepio. "Master Luke is going to blow a short circuit when he hears the news about the Emperor's son!"

"Tzoooooch briiiiiiiib!"

"Now what are you beeping about, you hysterical bag of bolts?"

SHIBOOOOOM!

Threepio looked up at the pink sky to see an Imperial command speeder that looked just like the one that was supposed to pick them up. But Artoo confirmed its number was not 714-D, so there was no reason to assume it was friendly.

And soon there wasn't just one command speeder, there were three—then four of them!

They seemed to be flying close to the mountains, looking for something.

Threepio began calculating the odds that they were searching for a certain meteor pod and two particular droids. He shook his head in dismay when he realized the chances were 1,245 to 1 that the Imperials had figured out they were there.

Threepio led Artoo behind a giant boulder, where they could peek out at the craggy, rocky meteor pod that had brought them to Kessel. But no sooner had the droids begun looking at their pod than a command speeder began shooting laserblasts at the surrounding boulders.

"I have a very bad feeling about this, Artoo," Threepio said grimly.

A blast suddenly struck the pod, exploding it into scrap metal right in front of the droids' eye-sensors.

"Oh, nooooooo!" said Threepio frantically.

Within moments, Threepio's bad feeling got

worse, as he watched an Imperial command speeder land near the exploded pod. Stormtroopers got out and began to inspect the debris.

"We're doomed," said Threepio.

"Get down, you two!" said a familiar-sounding voice.

Threepio turned and nearly stumbled in shock as a man in a green slave robe pulled back his hood and revealed his face.

"Master Luke! You found us. Oh, thank goodness! But what are you doing here?"

"Looking for you two. When there was no sign of your pod taking off, Admiral Ackbar and I figured you droids might be in need of some help. We took a big gamble by landing. Quick—this way!"

The droids followed Luke Skywalker into the Kesselian mountain forest. Moments later they ar-

rived at the Imperial command speeder that the Alliance had captured—Command Speeder 714-D—which was waiting for them.

Once they were safely inside, they greeted Admiral Ackbar, who was at the controls, and quickly blasted off.

The other Imperial command speeders followed them, firing at them from behind.

Ackbar and Luke returned the fire. They made a series of spectacular direct hits. One after another their enemies made crash dives, spinning out of control, back to the surface of Kessel.

As their spaceship soared away from the outer atmosphere of Kessel, Artoo's radar screen popped up and spun around quickly. *"Bzzz tzzzt gniiiz bzheeep dzz dzooop!"* he beeped urgently.

"Oh, dear," said Threepio. "Artoo definitely doesn't advise that we chart a direct course back to Yavin Four. He's spotted Imperial probe droids directly in our path!"

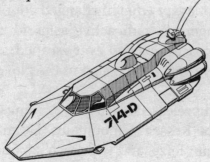

CHAPTER 4
Endangered Whaladons

Hundreds of probe droids with clawlike arms searched through space for the glove of Darth Vader.

While he waited for the reports from these probe droids, Trioculus delayed moving the Imperial forces to the bleak ice world of Hoth.

Soon news began trickling in.

The probe droids found everything but what Trioculus wanted most. They found debris from the Death Star, runaway prisoners, unexploded bombs, Alliance starships, and bounty hunters who were stealing Imperial weapons. They even spotted the missing Imperial Command Speeder 714-D, which narrowly got away when it changed course and entered a dangerous, radioactive asteroid zone from which few spaceships had ever escaped.

But there was still no sign of the glove of Darth Vader.

Trioculus released his fury by hunting giant fefze beetles in the Kesselian mountains. He managed to kill three giant fefze, and with each conquest Grand Moff Hissa congratulated him enthusiastically.

But still Trioculus wasn't satisfied. In an angry

voice he spoke of wanting a bigger hunt, a bigger kill. He proposed a journey to the steaming, ammonia-filled jungles of the planet Cona to hunt star dragons. However, before Grand Moff Hissa could even ask about arranging such a safari, Trioculus quickly changed the subject.

"Have any more troops questioned my right to be the new Emperor?" he asked.

"Some of the stormtroopers have been heard to complain, Lord Trioculus," replied Grand Moff Hissa.

"I want their names," Trioculus boomed, exploding with anger. "Their treason shall be punished!"

"Yes, your lordship." Grand Moff Hissa searched his mind for something new to report. "I also thought you should know that a salvage spaceship found what was thought to be a glove this morning. Unfortunately it turned out to be nothing but an old, rusted droid hand, floating in space in a cloud of hydrogen gas."

"Don't speak to me of droid hands, Hissa," said Trioculus, sneering. "My patience for this search is nearing an end."

Shortly after they returned to Trioculus's sleek black palace, a shipment of Whaladon meat was delivered to the palace kitchen. The delivery agent had come directly from the Kessel spaceport, where the meat had arrived in an Imperial carrack cruiser filled with cargo from the planet Calamari.

The agent bowed before Grand Moff Hissa, who accepted the delivery papers.

"I've also brought a message for Lord Trioculus from Captain Dunwell," said the delivery agent. He broke the seal on the small case he was carrying, took out a hologram disk, and handed it to Grand Moff Hissa, who in turn handed it over directly to Trioculus.

"See that no one disturbs me while I find out what Captain Dunwell has to say," ordered the three-eyed ruler.

Trioculus took the disk into one of his private chambers and inserted it into a holo-projector. Within moments the face of Captain Dunwell appeared as a holographic image, floating before him.

Captain Dunwell had a short white beard and a reddish, leathery face. He wore a blue naval uniform with shiny buttons and rows of medals.

"Dark Greetings, Lord Trioculus," he began. "Here, beneath the oceans of Calamari, I have made an astounding discovery. The Central Committee of Grand Moffs instructed me to contact you directly about this matter. As you may know, I have always been a loyal friend of the grand moffs. I urge you to come to see me on Calamari at once, at the Whaladon Processing Center. Your lordship will not be disappointed!"

Beneath the oceans of Calamari, Leviathor, the huge, white leader of the Whaladons, swam to the newly created Whaladon graveyard. In just a few years the bones of so many Whaladons had been dumped there by Captain Dunwell's Whaladon hunters that the sea floor in that region was now white.

Leviathor beheld the jagged rim of a crater just beyond the seaweed forest. Even from afar he could hear the dreaded machines churning in the huge underwater building at the bottom of that crater. The building was known as the Whaladon Processing Center.

Leviathor knew all too well that it was here where Captain Dunwell and his walrus-faced crew of Aqualish aliens killed the Whaladons that they captured.

There were now many young Whaladons who had no mothers to nurse them. And there were many older Whaladons, who used to swim the oceans of Calamari freely, who now hid, fearing for their

lives, in the darkness of undersea caves.

Swishing his great tail fin, Leviathor felt an invisible fire burning within him as he remembered the many learned and wise Whaladons who were now gone forever. No longer would they teach or sing songs—there was nothing left of them but their bones. Leviathor knew he had to save his endangered species before it was too late.

Just then a bright yellow light flashed behind Leviathor. He had been targeted. They were coming for *him* now!

The mighty Whaladon turned in the water and saw the huge new vessel—the biggest Whaladon-

hunting submarine ever built—tracking him, following him with his every dive.

Leviathor raced for his life, his huge heart pounding fast.

There was a roar behind him and the water swirled with foam. A great suction was pulling at his tail, suction as if from a whirlpool.

Leviathor dove again. Swimming as he had never swum before, he sailed into the seaweed forest and down into a wide coral cave.

There he hid until the death machine had passed by. Then Leviathor swam toward the Domed City of Aquarius, the undersea center of civilization on Calamari. He had to find someone who could help the Whaladons, and soon!

Aboard Command Speeder 714-D the recently installed shield that protected the spaceship against radioactivity did its job. It helped Luke and Admiral Ackbar navigate safely out of the dangerous asteroid zone, where they had maneuvered to get away from the prying eye-sensors of the Imperial probe droids.

"We'll go to Calamari, Luke," Admiral Ackbar said as he programmed the command speeder on an automatic course toward his home planet. "When we get there, we'll transfer Artoo-Detoo's spy data about Trioculus and the Imperial officers into a computer that will analyze it."

"But Mon Mothma and Princess Leia are waiting for that information *now*" said Luke.

"At the moment we're likely to be spotted by Imperials if we fly near Yavin Four," explained Ackbar. "We'll wait on Calamari for a while, then send a Calamarian cargo cruiser on ahead of us with the coded data."

"When we get to Calamari," Threepio asked anxiously, "will there be time for Artoo and me to be modified back to our usual-looking selves at the Droid Repair Shop in the Domed City of Aquarius?"

"Are you sure that's what you want, Threepio?" said Luke with a grin. "I'm sort of getting used to you being green—and mean-looking."

"Honestly, Master Luke, sometimes your sense of humor astounds me."

A short time later when they came out of hyperdrive in the region of Calamari, Admiral Ackbar contacted Pisces Base, one of the Calamarian cities on a platform that floated on the ocean. He alerted Pisces that Imperial Command Speeder 714-D was a friendly ship of the Alliance and requested permission to land.

From Pisces Base Admiral Ackbar took Luke, Threepio, and Artoo aboard a Calamarian shuttle submarine that was heading for the Domed City of Aquarius.

Though there were many other cities on platforms above the waters, the Domed City of Aquarius was the only one that was located entirely under the sea. It was encased in a gigantic bubble, with the lower half containing rocks, coral, canals, and seawater and the upper half containing air. In Aquarius air-breathers and water-breathers lived above and below one another, in a spirit of brotherhood and equality.

The Calamarian shuttle sub approached the domed city and entered the wide undersea tunnel entrance. Then it surfaced inside the bubble and docked.

As the spy mission team disembarked, Admiral Ackbar stopped suddenly. Luke wondered what was wrong. Finally Ackbar said, "Listen to that sound— it's a Whaladon song."

Luke noticed it, too. It was a faint, haunting melody, echoing between the tall buildings on both sides of the biggest canal in the city.

Making his way through the crowd, Ackbar led Luke and the droids toward the canal. There they saw Leviathor, his big white humps sticking out of the water.

Admiral Ackbar was one of the few air-breathing fishmen who understood Whaladon songs. As Leviathor sang about how the Whaladons were threatened with extinction because of Captain Dunwell's new Whaladon-hunting submarine, the admiral hung his head in sorrow.

"Wise One of the Calamarian Seas," said Admiral Ackbar, "you have my solemn promise that I will do everything I can to save you and your valiant species."

"Tell him he has my promise, too," Luke Skywalker added.

CHAPTER 5
Captain Dunwell's Discovery

Intent on learning what Captain Dunwell had found, Trioculus left for Calamari in an Imperial strike cruiser that had been modified to travel both in outer space and undersea.

Soon after the strike cruiser penetrated the atmosphere of Calamari, it plunged underwater. In the cruiser's forward observation room Trioculus peered with all three of his eyes at the misty, dark ocean bottom.

He could make out the outline of a crater. And moments later, inside the crater on the ocean floor, he could see the faint white outline of Captain Dunwell's Whaladon Processing Center.

"We're in contact with Captain Dunwell, sir," said Grand Moff Hissa. "He's planning to greet you with a thirty laser-cannon salute and a military procession."

"Absolutely not," said Trioculus in a stern voice. "If I had wanted to be noticed, I would have asked for a parade, not a private meeting."

"As you wish, my Emperor."

As the Imperial strike cruiser approached the

Whaladon Processing Center, Trioculus could see Captain Dunwell's new, immense Whaladon-hunting submarine stationed at an open undersea docking bay.

"It's equipped with whirlpool generators," explained Grand Moff Hissa, "for sucking the Whaladons right out of the ocean and into big storage chambers. The generators are powered by an antimatter furnace,"

"Impressive," said Trioculus.

As the Imperial strike cruiser entered another of the docking bays at the huge underwater facility, Grand Moff Hissa assisted Trioculus's crew with the docking procedures.

GRONGGGG!

A clang sounded as a large metal door closed behind Trioculus's Imperial strike cruiser. Then seawater was quickly pumped out of the docking bay, making it safe for Trioculus, Grand Moff Hissa, and the droid Emdee to climb out and enter the Whaladon Processing Center.

There they were met by Captain Dunwell, who knelt on one knee and bowed his head before the Imperial leader. "Lord Trioculus," he said, "a most Imperial welcome to you." Then he glanced up and smiled proudly.

Trioculus didn't like the way the captain seemed to be staring at him. It was as though the captain were repulsed by Trioculus's third eye.

"I trust you had a safe and comfortable journey," Captain Dunwell offered, nervously tweaking his short white beard.

"You need not worry about my comfort," replied Trioculus. "I want to know what was so urgent that I had to come all the way to Calamari for you to show it to me."

"Certainly, your lordship," said the captain, fidgeting with the medals on his bright blue uniform. "Come, we should speak in the privacy of my office."

Together they climbed up some stairs, then walked along a metal balcony that overlooked an enormous work area. Down below, dozens of Aqualish were skinning several Whaladons that had been killed, chopping the meat into huge slabs and loading it into carts.

The walrus-faced alien race of Aqualish, who had smooth, tough skins and large eyes, was a stubborn and tough fighting breed. They worked as bounty hunters, mercenaries, and as ruthless Whaladon killers.

The Whaladon meat they were chopping would soon be transported to the Whaladon Meat Quality Control Division.

Trioculus's three eyes peered down at the workers as he walked slowly from one end of the balcony to the other. He nodded approvingly, but his mind was on other things. In fact, he was in such an impatient mood that his right hand had begun twitching.

"I hope you're finding this instructive," said Captain Dunwell. "My office is just a little farther."

They continued walking through cold corridors and across wide work platforms until they reached the building's largest office, which belonged to Captain Dunwell. It had a gigantic window with a wide, sweeping view of the ocean and its enormous seaweed forest containing exotic Calamarian fish of every size, color, and shape imaginable.

When the Imperial leader entered the office, followed by Grand Moff Hissa and Emdee, Captain Dunwell locked the door and pointed to a navigation chart.

"This chart shows the route I took when I made my last journey to the Valley of the Giant Oysters, located on the other side of the Seascape Mountains. And this area here," Captain Dunwell continued, pointing out a small region of the undersea valley, "is where I discovered debris from an explosion."

The captain showed Trioculus the few metal scraps that were on his desk. "This is some of the debris I brought back with me. I've had it analyzed by an engineer—it's from the Death Star. I could hardly believe it since the Death Star blew up millions of miles away, near Endor."

"The intense gravity of black holes and other interstellar forces cause warps, folds, and buckles in space," explained Grand Moff Hissa. "Asteroids and spaceships have tumbled into these space warps and have suddenly reappeared millions of miles away. The same thing must have happened to this debris from the Imperial Death Star."

"Enough theories, Hissa," said Trioculus. "Continue with your story, Captain Dunwell."

He stared at the captain with his third eye, sending out hypnotic waves. A stare like that could make a man very truthful. The captain turned slightly pale.

"One of the chunks of the Death Star lying in the valley was huge—bigger than a Y-wing fighter, all melted and fused in a twisted shape. It was too large to bring back in the vessel I was in, so I suited up and examined it on the ocean floor. I tried to blast a hole in it, but my small laser couldn't do the job.

"I suspected that it was hollow, so I used my portable X-ray scanner to find out what was inside," he went on. "Allow me to show you what the scanner revealed."

The captain opened a drawer and took out several X-ray negatives. He studied first one image, then another, and then another. "Here," he said at last. "Look at this one." He touched his forefinger to the shadowy negative.

Trioculus leaned forward for a closer look.

Shutting his two lower eyes, he stared at the image with his third eye. The spot that Captain Dunwell was touching showed an object that seemed to have five fingers. Was it a hand? Or a glove?

Trioculus glanced at his right hand, which was trembling once again as he dreamed of fulfilling his goal. No human hand could have survived the heat of the Death Star explosion, he thought. And only one glove was known to be totally indestructible. This had to be it. A short undersea journey away. Almost within his grasp.

"You were correct to request that I come here, Captain," said Trioculus. "You have done well."

"Thank you, your lordship," said the captain, his voice booming with pride.

"How soon can you get us to the Valley of the Giant Oysters?" asked Grand Moff Hissa.

"I'll tell my crew to power up the Whaladon-hunting submarine immediately," Captain Dunwell replied.

Even sooner than Trioculus had expected, they were ready to depart.

KRR-RR—AAAAAAANG!

With a mighty roar the Whaladon-hunting submarine pushed away from its undersea dock. Bubbling foam churned behind it as the huge submarine picked up speed.

Captain Dunwell pointed out to Trioculus each of the vessel's special features.

Trioculus's face darkened with a nasty smile. "With so much advanced technology aboard, you'll have to make sure this ship is never captured by the Rebel Alliance."

"Have no fear of that, Lord Trioculus," replied Captain Dunwell. "If there's ever an undersea battle on Calamari, I'll destroy this ship myself before I'll ever let it fall into the hands of the Rebels."

* * *

Luke Skywalker's heart was pounding with excitement as Threepio translated Artoo's high-pitched beeps. All of Artoo's intelligence data about the meeting of Imperials in Kessendra Stadium was now at Luke's fingertips.

Luke and Admiral Ackbar soon hurried to the Calamarian office of SPIN. For months Luke had received intelligence reports about the Empire's many denials concerning the rumor that Emperor Palpatine had had a son. But at the big Imperial meeting in Kessendra Stadium the Empire had suddenly admitted that all its denials had been false. Just thinking about it made Luke shake his head in frustration. How could anyone believe *anything* the Empire said, when the Empire changed the "official truth" day by day to suit its convenience?

While Luke and Admiral Ackbar took care of the urgent business of contacting Mon Mothma about Trioculus, Threepio and Artoo checked into the Droid Repair Shop.

Threepio was given another head cover that was exactly like his old one, except that this one was shinier, without any scratches, nicks, or dents. He admired his replating job, looking at his golden color from every angle.

Artoo-Detoo also underwent a change back to his usual color. But it was his brand-new blue and silver R2 dome that made the little barrel-shaped droid spin in circles, showing how happy he was to be back to normal.

When the droids came out of the Droid Repair Shop, Luke, Threepio, and Artoo boarded a fish-shaped Calamarian minisub with Admiral Ackbar, who navigated the vessel toward the ocean floor.

"Now that we've sent the news to Mon Mothma about the Imperial leader Trioculus, it's time we tried to help the Whaladons," Ackbar told them. "And the best way for me to explain the Whaladon crisis is to show you the Whaladon graveyard. From there it's a short trip to Captain Dunwell's undersea Whaladon Processing Center."

"Dzneeeeek?" beeped Artoo.

"Artoo wants to know what they do there," translated Threepio.

"That's where they take the captured Whaladons and butcher them," said Admiral Ackbar. "There they turn those beautiful, intelligent creatures into food for Imperial officers!"

"Perish the thought," said Threepio, shaking his head in dismay.

"For many years we've had a law on Calamari making it illegal to hunt Whaladons," explained Admiral Ackbar. "But no matter how hard we try we cannot control Captain Dunwell. He does whatever the Central Committee of Grand Moffs wants, and they want Whaladon meat, even if it means destroying the ecology of Calamari."

"Chnooozbch kjiiiik?" beeped Artoo.

"Artoo wants to know how the hunting of Whaladons harms the ecology of your planet,"

Threepio translated.

"The Whaladons eat the little plants, or plankton, that grow at the surface of our oceans," Ackbar explained. "If those little plants spread and become too plentiful, as they breathe they could use up all the carbon dioxide in our atmosphere—the process of photosynthesis. Without carbon dioxide our planet would get much colder. You see, we need Whaladons to keep the amount of plankton in balance, or we Calamarians could wake up one day to find ourselves in an ice age!"

Admiral Ackbar's attention was suddenly captured by a blip on his sonar unit. "Luke, have a look at this," he said in a serious tone. He pointed to a bright circle of luminous light on the sonar screen. "The only vessel of this size in these waters is Captain Dunwell's submarine. Let's see what he's up to."

Cautiously the Calamarian minisub followed the huge, dark shape lurking dead ahead. Light from luminous coral began reflecting off the Whaladon-hunting submarine, making its dark form more vis-

ible. Luke could see that the vessel was like a vast self-propelled underwater fortress.

The Calamarian minisub followed it silently, navigating the same course at a safe distance to the rear. The small size and efficient antisonar system of the Calamarian minisub made it almost impossible for an enemy to detect, except at very close range.

In the cramped cabin Luke Skywalker watched through the front porthole. Threepio was tightly strapped into the rear seat, beneath the emergency navigation controls, and Artoo was pushed up against the golden droid's knees.

Luke could see the white form of Leviathor leading a group of Whaladons away from the path of the dreaded submarine. Then he choked with horror as he saw a swirling mass of foaming dark water, like an undersea tornado, moving straight toward Leviathor.

Admiral Ackbar struggled to control his little sub as it vibrated wildly in the churning water. Luke watched as Leviathor tried to escape, but the whirlpool caught hold of Leviathor as the old white Whaladon fought for his life.

The suction pulled Leviathor backward, tail first. Then Leviathor spun around and around at a dizzying speed, while a huge door opened on the side of the Whaladon-hunting submarine. In a few moments Leviathor was sucked through the door and he vanished from sight.

THUUUU-WHOMP!

As the metal door slammed shut, claiming its

prize catch, Luke could hear a dull thud pounding through the waves.

"This is a very sad day for Calamari," said Ackbar, shuddering. "Without Leviathor the Whaladons haven't a chance now."

Luke's mouth fell open as he saw another Whaladon trapped in the whirlpool. The Whaladon fell into the swirling hole, tumbling and twisting, then was quickly trapped inside another storage chamber.

Then a third Whaladon was trapped.

And a fourth.

Ackbar abruptly pushed the steering lever to the left. Their Calamarian minisub turned sharply away, then picked up speed.

"Surely there must be something we can do," said Threepio, nervously polishing his fingers. "Why, they've swallowed up four Whaladons in the last few minutes, including Leviathor."

"It looks hopeless," said Ackbar sadly.

Luke remembered all of the hopeless situations he had been in before. How many times in his life had he almost been ready to give up? But he never had.

If there was any hope of saving the Whaladons, they couldn't turn back now. So they kept following the Whaladon-hunting submarine as it went straight toward the dark Seascape Mountains.

Luke squinted, almost losing sight of the huge vessel as the shadows of the undersea cliffs concealed it. But he could still just barely make it out in the darkening waters. It cruised toward a large passageway between two rugged underwater cliffs.

"There are no Whaladons this way—destination unknown," said Admiral Ackbar, wondering where Captain Dunwell was headed.

It was a dangerous journey through the jagged mountains that stretched across the bottom of the sea. There were hot currents that bubbled up and shook their Calamarian minisub, and there were falling rocks that tumbled through the water and almost crushed them.

When they finally emerged from a hollow space that formed a natural tunnel in the mountain, they reached a valley unlike any that Luke had ever seen. It was bathed in the soft green light of a luminous, flowery vine forest. Every few moments there were glints of color sparkling through the water, glows from alien eel creatures that lived and thrived in the depths of the Calamarian ocean. He stared in wonder at the eels and at the huge gleaming pearls, hundreds of them, inside the open mouths of the giant oysters on the valley floor.

Luke didn't know what surprised him more—the number of oysters or their size. Any one of them was large enough to swallow him with one quick bite.

But the pearls and slithering eel creatures weren't all that was gleaming. There was a glint from jagged edges that seemed to be scraps of metal.

Artoo's domed top swiveled around and his little radar screen popped up as high as it could go. He tooted and whistled.

"*Tweeeeez bziiiiii!*"

"Well, I do believe you're correct, Artoo," Threepio exclaimed. "It's like a mine field. There are pieces of metal debris everywhere."

"It looks like something exploded," said Admiral Ackbar. "Luke, can your Artoo unit examine a piece of metal and determine its atomic structure?"

"*Jizoookch!*" squawked Artoo.

"Affirmative, sir," Threepio explained.

"Let's use the arm-scoop then," said Ackbar.

Skillfully handling the control for the underwater arm-scoop, the admiral extended a long rod that had a metal claw at its end. The claw grabbed a small piece of scrap metal, then the rod was pulled back into their minisub.

In a moment a narrow slot popped open on the floor near Luke's right boot, revealing the piece of metal that the arm-scoop had just pulled out of the ocean.

Luke reached for it. "Here you go, Artoo," he said, holding it in front of his little utility droid. "Take a quick reading on this."

"I'm especially interested to know whether it contains any doonium or phobium," said Ackbar.

"*Gooooo-zizzz beee-zeeez!*" beeped Artoo.

Threepio translated Artoo's answer. The metal was six percent doonium, a very heavy element used by the Empire in most of its war machines. The metal was also three percent phobium.

"Phobium was mined by Emperor Palpatine on Gargon," said Ackbar. "And there's only one thing I know of that he ever used it for: to coat the power core of the Death Star."

Luke's eyes widened in astonishment. "So then these are scraps from the power core of the exploded Death Star!" He stared through the front porthole again. The Whaladon-hunting submarine had stopped.

A small sub that Luke guessed was an emergency-escape vehicle exited the Whaladon-hunting submarine. But now it was being used for exploration, not for escape.

Slowly and steadily it approached a large chunk of twisted scrap metal, one almost as large as an Imperial command speeder. Luke felt a shiver run up his spine as he suddenly realized what was about to happen.

CHAPTER 6
Ten Minutes to Self-Destruct

A hatch on the escape sub opened and Trioculus emerged alone, while Grand Moff Hissa and the others remained behind.

Trioculus wore a diving suit of the most advanced design, equipped with a helmet that had a miniature arc light. He took a supply of thermal detonators with him.

KABRAAAA-AAM!

The thermal detonators blasted a hole in the side of the large chunk of the Death Star sprawled across the ocean floor. Then Trioculus pulled himself through the hole into the big, hollow piece of metallic debris. He adjusted the arc light on his helmet so that he could examine the crushed mechanical parts that surrounded him.

He found a large lump that looked like the remains of a melted energy dish. He also found a maze of mashed turbolaser cooling tubes and ion equalizers, scorched and clumped together so that they were almost unrecognizable.

And then his third eye noticed three black fingertips sticking out from beneath a mashed ion deactivator.

He pushed aside the ion deactivator, and there it was: a five-fingered black gauntlet, in one piece, undamaged by heat or water.

In fact, the glove looked just as it must have looked when Darth Vader had worn it on his right hand!

Luke bit his lower lip as he kept staring through the front porthole of the Calamarian minisub. Using underwater macrobinoculars, he could see that the diver had three eyes—Trioculus! The Imperial tyrant was reentering the escape sub, and Luke wondered whether Trioculus had just found the glove of Darth Vader.

"Ackbar, can we catch up with that little sub before it gets back inside the Whaladon-hunting submarine?" Luke asked.

"I don't see how," Ackbar replied somberly. "If we get too close, we'll be discovered. One blast from their laser cannons and we'll be finished."

"I say it's time to retreat then," said Threepio.

Luke remembered the words of Yoda, his Jedi teacher: *Luke, the coming fight is yours alone. There is no avoiding the battle—you cannot escape your destiny.*

"We're not going to retreat, Threepio," said Luke. He turned to the Calamarian fishman beside him. "Admiral Ackbar, is there any way we could signal Trioculus and communicate with him somehow?"

"You mean let him know that we're here?"

"Exactly. If we surrender to him, then he'll take us aboard to question us, right? But that will be the biggest mistake he'll ever make."

"Or the biggest one *we'll* ever make," said Ackbar.

Another thought struck Luke. "The other thing we could do is attack."

"Attack!" exclaimed Threepio.

It was an old Jedi rule of thumb to attack when the odds were overwhelmingly against you, and when there was no other possible way to save your own life or the life of an ally. Luke had used that strategy aboard Jabba the Hutt's skiff when Luke and his friends were about to be executed.

"Ackbar, let's get closer to them," said Luke. "Full speed ahead."

"Full speed ahead," repeated Admiral Ackbar reluctantly.

"Oh, dear, I do hope you know what you're doing, Master Luke," said Threepio in a whining voice. "Don't say I didn't warn you—"

Admiral Ackbar pushed hard on the overdrive booster, making their Calamarian minisub go at maximum speed.

FAZHOOOOM!

Their sub lurched forward in the water, then the power suddenly failed. It was totally dark.

"I tried to accelerate faster than we can go, triggering a systems shutdown," said Ackbar. "Threepio, reach up and put your hand on the emergency control lever just above your head. And yank hard."

Threepio did as he was told. The backup generator turned on, and an emergency steering unit popped out of the ceiling, practically landing in Threepio's lap.

"Just push up on that red knob, Threepio," Ackbar continued.

"Pushing as instructed," said Threepio. "Oh, dear."

"Now just hold it steady and steer us on a straight course. The main pilot control should automatically switch on again in about one minute."

"But I haven't the faintest idea how to pilot this thing," Threepio protested.

"It's easy, even a housekeeping droid could do it," said Ackbar. "Just hold that red knob steady."

Threepio tried his best, but the Calamarian minisub tilted on its side, then flipped upside down and plunged straight for the bottom. Then, just seconds before it was about to smash on some rocks, he pulled it out of its nosedive.

"*Bzeeech! Chnooooch!*" beeped Artoo frantically.

"Well, you try to steer it, then, if you think you're so smart," said Threepio. "Hmmph. 'Even a housekeeping droid could do it'!"

At that moment the main pilot control switched back on and Admiral Ackbar took over once again.

"If I could make a suggestion, Master Luke," said Threepio, "I *really* think we ought to head back. We can return to see the sights down here some other time."

"*Zgoonukooo!*" squealed Artoo.

"Yikes!" shouted Threepio. "A giant squid!"

He was right. Luke glanced out the front port-hole and saw a squid larger than any he could ever have imagined. It had long, writhing, twisting ten-tacles with big, grotesque suction cups. The squid jetted through the water just overhead and passed them.

Suddenly the Whaladon-hunting submarine cre-ated another whirlpool, which churned like an angry tornado, going right toward the squid.

FWISHHHHH!

The squid was caught in the whirlpool, but then so was the Calamarian minisub! Around and around they spun, tumbling and falling as they felt the whirl-pool sucking them through the opening of a storage chamber right along with the giant squid.

"Oh, nooooo!" shouted Threepio. "Master Luke, we're dooooomed!"

* * *

No one aboard the Whaladon-hunting submarine even realized that the Calamarian minisub had been sucked into the hold along with the giant squid.

The crew members were more concerned with a game that had just begun, a gambling game known as sabacc. Sabacc was a card game that had become very popular in the casinos of Cloud City on Bespin, and now it was played by both humans and aliens on dozens of planets.

A few Aqualish with big tusks began the game, and soon they were joined by others, as they crouched in the main corridor not far from the decompression chamber.

But the game wasn't going smoothly. The Aqualish began growling and pushing, calling each other cheaters and opening their mouths, flashing their teeth and tusks, even spitting at one another.

Trioculus, whose body had just returned to its normal pressure, came out of the decompression chamber. With his black uniform properly in place again, he turned his attention to the glove of Darth Vader.

The droid Emdee had cleaned away the grime and then brought the black glove back to his master, whose right hand trembled as he reached for it. Trioculus put the glove on slowly, regally, like a king setting a crown on his head. An image of Darth Vader flashed into Trioculus's mind, and at that instant the evil of Vader seemed to pour through him like a sudden surge of power from the Dark Side.

"It fits your hand perfectly, your lordship," said Grand Moff Hissa, flattering Trioculus, "as though it were made for you to wear!"

They proceeded to Captain Dunwell's cabin.

When they approached the part of the corridor where the sabacc game was being played, Grand Moff Hissa cautioned Trioculus, telling him that the noisy Aqualish gamblers in their path seemed to be out of control.

As Trioculus drew closer, the gang of Aqualish didn't even look up, let alone step out of his way. They were as rude and stupid as any Aqualish he had ever encountered anywhere in the galaxy.

Grand Moff Hissa clicked his heels to get their attention. "Why aren't you Aqualish at your work stations?" he demanded.

But there was no reply, only a snarling growl from the loser and a coarse laugh from the winner as he picked up his credit chips. Trioculus's three eyes turned fiery.

"You are blocking the path of the Supreme Ruler of the Empire!" Grand Moff Hissa shouted. "Clear a path and get back to work now or you'll all be executed!"

The one with the thickest tusks just sneered, then spit on the floor and hissed at the Imperials.

"How dare you!" an enraged Trioculus boomed, raising the glove of Darth Vader and pointing it at the Aqualish who had just insulted him.

But to Trioculus's amazement nothing happened.

The glove didn't work for him the way it had worked for Darth Vader, who had been able to choke the life-breath out of his victims by pointing the glove in their direction.

Scowling, Trioculus raised his other hand and lightning bolts flowed from his fingertips, causing the offending Aqualish to crumple to the ground, kicking and writhing. The electricity quickly reduced him to an unrecognizable heap.

The remaining Aqualish scattered at once, without any further incident. Moments later Trioculus, Grand Moff Hissa, and Emdee arrived at the captain's private quarters.

Captain Dunwell agreed to depart so that the Imperial leader could confer with his most trusted advisors without being disturbed.

Shaking his head in disgust, Trioculus sat down in the captain's favorite chair. "When Darth Vader pointed this glove, he had the power to choke his victims," he said. "The glove is useless if it no longer has that power."

"The important thing to remember," said Grand Moff Hissa, "is that the glove is a great symbol of evil. As we know, the Supreme Prophet of the Dark Side, Kadann, prophesied that the new Emperor would wear that glove. And now that you wear it, none of the Imperial warlords can question your claim to be our new Emperor. And Kadann won't be able to question your authority, either, once we go to Space Station Scardia and prove to him that you have found it."

"I'm not interested in *symbols*," said Trioculus. "I want the same power as Darth Vader!"

Grand Moff Hissa continued. "My lord, you must realize that, though you are a great slavelord, it could still take many years for you to become a True Master of the Dark Side. Don't forget, the lightning bolts don't flow naturally from your fingertips like they did with Emperor Palpatine. Emdee had to implant a cybernetic device inside of you so that you could appear to have the lightning power. But if you use it too many times, all that electricity could prove fatal to you. You mustn't use it anymore. Fortunately, however, the lightning device has already served its purpose. It helped us to convince everyone that you *are* the Emperor's son, which is exactly what the Central Committee of Grand Moffs wanted to do."

"Never forget," Trioculus said with a blaze of anger in all three of his eyes, "that when the Central Committee of Grand Moffs proposed to me that I be the one to declare himself the Emperor's son, you grand moffs swore you would keep the plot a secret. And in turn I agreed that when I became Emperor, I would share my rule with the Central Committee of Grand Moffs."

"And I hope *you* shall never forget," said Grand Moff Hissa, bearing his pointy teeth, "that we dreamed up this plot only because we had absolutely no choice. The Emperor's real three-eyed son, Triclops, is hopelessly insane, and all of our attempts to cure him have met with failure. Obviously it's better that a trusted three-eyed mutant, such as yourself, should take his place, my lord. If we were to permit Triclops to rule the Empire, his madness would surely bring about the end of us all!"

Emdee removed a small utility case from his left side. He opened the case, then carefully took out five very tiny mechanisms, each the size of a man's fingertip.

"I can put one of these inside the tip of each of the glove's fingers," Emdee said, holding one of them up. "When your fingers press against these devices, they will give off a piercing, high-frequency sound, an earsplitting pitch heard only by the one you've aimed the glove at. It will make your victims gasp and fall to their knees. Their eardrums will explode and their brains disintegrate, just like Darth Vader was able to do with his own natural power."

* * *

Luke stared through a minisub window down at the giant squid, which lay almost lifeless in a huge, cube-shaped Whaladon storage chamber. He breathed a sigh of relief that the squid had been stunned into a state of unconsciousness by the whirlpool. However, there was no relief at all for him when he realized that the minisub was trapped inside the same storage chamber as the squid. Although Luke, Admiral Ackbar, and the two droids were safe for the moment, they had to find a way out—fast.

Ackbar piloted their minisub to the top of the storage chamber, which was filled with seawater. Then he attached their sub magnetically to a hatch that led into the main corridor of the Whaladon-hunting submarine. Artoo sent an electronic signal that caused the hatch to pop open.

"Good work, Artoo," said Luke. "Admiral Ackbar, I think you should wait here and be ready in case we need to make a quick escape."

Moments later Luke, Artoo, and Threepio walked cautiously down the corridor. Passing several other Whaladon storage chambers, they looked down into them and saw a trapped Whaladon in each.

Then they saw the chamber where Leviathor was imprisoned. Leviathor was flapping his tail aimlessly, moaning sadly.

Luke spied Captain Dunwell, who was standing alone, armed with a standard blaster, staring down at Leviathor. Luke recognized Dunwell immediately from the WANTED holograms that Ackbar had projected for him.

The captain was stroking his beard. He was deeply disturbed because he had overheard the conversation between Trioculus, Grand Moff Hissa, and Emdee. Captain Dunwell had deliberately bugged his own quarters with hidden microphones. And Trioculus, in his haste to find a private place to talk, had forgotten to have Grand Moff Hissa check for any listening devices.

The captain now knew some very dark and dangerous secrets. But what should he do with this information?

As Captain Dunwell glanced up, he suddenly noticed Luke, Threepio, and Artoo. He pulled out his blaster and fired two short blasts, one of which struck Artoo and sent the little droid spinning around and around in a circle.

Luke instantly drew his lightsaber. He struck the

blade against Captain Dunwell's blaster, and the weapon tumbled out of the captain's hand.

"Who are you?" the captain demanded. "And how did you get on board this ship?"

"I'm asking the questions and giving the orders now, Captain," said Luke. "And here's order number one. You're going to find us a computer terminal so we can hook up with this ship's master control system."

"A computer terminal won't do you any good," replied the captain. "You could *never* decipher our data codes."

"I seriously doubt that Artoo here will have any problem with your codes," said Luke.

"Kill me if you want. But I'll never help you!"

Using a Jedi mind trick that Obi-Wan Kenobi had taught him, Luke looked Captain Dunwell straight in the eyes and said, "You've mistaken us for your enemies."

"I've mistaken you for my enemies," a dazed Captain Dunwell repeated in a soft voice.

"You wanted us to come here so we could help you."

"I wanted you to come here," said the captain.

"We're supposed to check your master control," said Luke, continuing to use his Jedi mind power. "Now take us to a computer terminal quickly."

"I will take you to a terminal."

The captain lead them up one corridor and down another. Finally he showed them to a computer terminal.

"Artoo," said Luke, "hook into this terminal and figure out how to crack the communication code. Then instruct the ship's master control to open the doors to the Whaladon storage chambers. Let all the Whaladons free!"

Artoo extended a little metal arm and hooked himself into the computer terminal.

"You fool," said Captain Dunwell, recovering his senses. "You think that little utility droid of yours can crack a code I spent three years creating?"

"*Gaaaaaz booop dweeet!*" beeped Artoo.

"He says you underestimate him, Captain," said Threepio. "He says Darth Vader's codes used to be *much* more complicated than yours, and it never took him more than fifteen seconds to figure *those* out."

"Artoo, I just thought of something," Luke said. "Before you free the Whaladons, the first thing you should do is scan the ship's data banks. Find out if this vessel has a self-destruct system."

"It doesn't," said Captain Dunwell.

"*Zuuuuung! Galooooop!*" squawked Artoo.

"Artoo says it does, Master Luke," Threepio confirmed.

"Excellent," said Luke. "Find out the precise self-destruct code. Tell me when you've got it."

"Trioculus expects me to be back in the navigation room by now," said Captain Dunwell. "If he comes looking for me and finds you, he'll destroy you instantly!"

"*Zoooosh-bee-dwee,*" beeped Artoo, rolling his

domed top around to show his excitement.

"He has the self-destruct code, Master Luke," explained Threepio.

"Good droid, Artoo. Now punch in the self-destruct code and set the ship to blow up in . . . "

Luke stopped to think. How much time would the Whaladons need to swim to a safe distance? And how much time would he, his droids, and Admiral Ackbar need to get their Calamarian minisub away from here without being destroyed by a gigantic explosion?

"Give us ten minutes—that should do it," said Luke. "And if it doesn't, well then we're all history."

"You can't do this!" Captain Dunwell protested.

Artoo beeped and squeaked and whirred. *"Booooshsh! Zweeech!"*

"Artoo says yes we can," Threepio translated. "Just watch us."

"Ziiish bajoooop!" Artoo tooted.

"Self-destruct is activated, Master Luke!" reported Threepio.

Just then alarm bells started to go off and warning lights blinked along the corridor.

CHAPTER 7
The Captain's Reward

"Quick, Artoo!" said Luke. "Tell the master control to free the Whaladons!"

"He's searching for a way to do it, Master Luke," said Threepio. "He's looking and—oh, gracious, he can't find it! Keep looking, Artoo. We've got to save Leviathor and the other Whaladons before—"

Suddenly Trioculus appeared down at the end of the hall. "Oh, no, Master Luke, Trioculus has found us!" Threepio shouted. "We're doomed!"

"Your droid has grasped your situation well, Skywalker," said Trioculus. He raised his gloved right hand and pointed it at Luke. "Now prepare to die!" he shouted.

Luke ducked behind Captain Dunwell. Gripping the captain, Luke positioned him directly in front of the glove of Darth Vader.

Captain Dunwell gasped as a high-pitched deadly sound vibration struck him. Luke then lifted the captain and heaved him, making him collide with Trioculus and toppling them both to the floor. Then Luke drew out his lightsaber.

"Jeeep booo poooooz!" tooted Artoo.

"Success!" shouted Threepio. "Artoo has instructed the master control to free the Whaladons!"

Just then the doors of the Whaladon storage chambers began to open. All the while the alarm bells were getting louder and the warning lights were flashing faster. Time was getting short before the Whaladon-hunting submarine would self-destruct in a furious explosion that would destroy them all.

Trioculus raised his left hand, electricity crackling from his fingertips. Luke met the electric bolt with his lightsaber, deflecting it. Trioculus's eyes bulged and his chest froze, as the warning of Grand Moff Hissa flooded back into his mind. The lightning power would be the death of him if he continued to use it. He was not yet a True Master of the Dark Side, not yet able to absorb intense electric shock without experiencing side effects.

But Trioculus allowed the flow of electricity to increase, aiming the bolts so that they would avoid Luke's lightsaber blade and strike him directly in the chest.

Luke crumpled to the ground, writhing on the floor as he felt the full force of the powerful jolts. Trioculus continued to pour bolts of electricity from his fingertips until Luke had stopped stirring. Then he lowered his hand and spoke rapidly into a pocket communication device. "Hissa, power up the escape sub! Quickly!"

Hissa's reply came from the device. "We'll need Captain Dunwell's key card to power it up!"

Trioculus turned to the captain. "Hand me your key card for the escape sub! At once!"

By the time Trioculus had snatched the key card from Captain Dunwell's hand, Luke Skywalker was back on his feet and was running down the corridor that would lead him to the Calamarian minisub.

"You may have escaped from Emperor Palpatine, but I shall destroy you, Skywalker!" Trioculus shouted. "You have my promise!"

Luke kept running—all the way back to the Calamarian minisub. He crawled through the hatch and saw that Threepio and Admiral Ackbar were already strapped into their seats waiting for him, and Artoo was in position, too.

They began their escape. The giant squid was just beginning to stir as Ackbar deftly navigated their Calamarian minisub over its slowly writhing body. A tentacle nearly grabbed them, but Ackbar successfully steered a course through the open door of the storage chamber and into the ocean depths.

As they sailed away, Luke looked out the window and saw Leviathor leading the freed Whaladons back through the Seascape Mountains, swimming as fast as their fins would take them.

Trioculus reached the escape sub with only two minutes remaining until the self-destruct system would blast the Whaladon-hunting submarine apart. Emdee and Grand Moff Hissa were waiting for him. Captain Dunwell arrived breathless seconds later.

"Let me get aboard first so I can warm up the ion thrusters," said the captain as Trioculus inserted the key card into the lock of the escape sub's door.

"Just a moment," replied Grand Moff Hissa, standing in his way. "No one enters the escape sub before the Supreme Ruler of the Empire, the True Master of the Dark Side."

Captain Dunwell turned to face Trioculus. "And *are* you the True Master of the Dark Side?" said Captain Dunwell without thinking. "I thought a Master of the Dark Side didn't need to rely on mechanical devices to give him lightning power or to make the glove of Darth—"

He stopped in mid-sentence, his face turning pale as he realized he had said too much about things he wasn't supposed to know.

"Out of my way," snapped Trioculus, glaring at the captain.

As Trioculus began to climb into the escape sub, he felt a stabbing pain in his eyes. For a second everything went black, but then he pressed his forehead, blinked a few times, and the momentary loss of vision went away. He could see again, and he hastily strapped himself into a seat.

Grand Moff Hissa climbed in, too, followed by Emdee.

But when Captain Dunwell tried to join them, the Imperial ruler stared at him with a piercing hypnotic glare and said calmly, "You know the procedure, Captain. In the Empire the captain always goes down with his ship."

"Lord Trioculus, I led you to the glove of Darth Vader!" said Captain Dunwell, nervously tweaking his beard. "I thought you would show some appreciation. Is death to be my reward?"

"I don't reward men who spy on me, Captain."

"Lord Trioculus, please have mercy, let me aboard— "

As Trioculus pointed the glove of Darth Vadar at him, Captain Dunwell tried to shut out the piercing sound that suddenly assaulted his eardrums. The captain's eyes then twirled upward as he let out a hoarse gasp, fell to his knees, and then dropped to the floor.

Hissa kicked the door shut and locked it. Leaving Captain Dunwell behind to die with his crew, the escape sub pushed away from the Whaladon-hunting submarine, making its way higher in the ocean as it sailed toward the dim outline of the undersea mountain range.

Moments later the escape sub shook violently as a tremendous explosion tore apart the Whaladon-hunting submarine, sending scraps of scorched metal spinning through the sea in all directions.

An evil smile spread across Trioculus's face as he clenched his gloved right hand into a fist. That hand no longer twitched. It now felt strong, invincible—and ready to rule the galaxy!

Luke's adventure had led him back to the place where it all began—on Yavin Four, where Luke and his droids were now gathered in the Alliance Senate. They had just finished delivering a complete report to SPIN on all that they had accomplished on their mission.

Luke, Threepio, and Artoo were congratulated by SPIN, not just for their espionage on Kessel but for their help in saving the Whaladons.

When the meeting had adjourned and most of the SPIN members departed, Admiral Ackbar turned to Luke, Threepio, Artoo, and Princess Leia and said, "On behalf of the planet Calamari, as a special thanks, I'd like to invite you all to be our guests of honor at a special concert of Whaladon songs at our Domed City of Aquarius."

"Fzzzzoooop bedoooooop!" squeaked Artoo in a scolding tone.

"I'm very sorry to report," Threepio said in a disappointed voice, "that Artoo absolutely *refuses*

ever to return to Calamari with me again—that is, until I get a license to steer a Calamarian minisub!"

Luke laughed, remembering that Threepio's brief moments of piloting the minisub had almost been the death of them. However, with a little coaxing from Luke, Artoo was persuaded to change his mind.

Sure enough, when the day of the Whaladon concert arrived, Luke and his friends were once again on Calamari, seated in the aquatheater in the Domed City of Aquarius.

The program of Whaladon songs was spectacular. It included a water ballet, Whaladon folk melodies, classical Whaladon songs, and an opera Leviathor had composed that told the legendary story of how he had become the Whaladon leader many years ago by helping the Whaladons survive an undersea volcanic eruption.

As much as Luke enjoyed the concert, being back on Calamari made him think about those final fateful moments before the Whaladon-hunting submarine had exploded, when he had glanced back and noticed the Imperial escape sub departing.

Had that escape sub been destroyed by the hurtling debris? Or had Trioculus survived, making it back to the planet's watery surface so that he could live to fight another day?

Try as he might to forget the Imperial leader's dire threat, Luke was unable to banish from his mind Trioculus's parting words: *"I shall destroy you, Skywalker! You have my promise!"*

To find out more about Luke Skywalker and SPIN's plans for the Empire, don't miss *The Lost City of the Jedi*, book two of our continuing Star Wars adventures.

Here's a preview:

In his dream, Luke saw himself on a secret mission, zooming along on his airspeeder. He was close above the treetops of the rain forest—and then suddenly the forest burst into flames, with smoke rising up all around him. Luke was coughing, choking, losing control of his airspeeder.

It tumbled down into the burning foliage. Luke fell off, plunging through the vines and thick leaves. He landed with a thud on the forest floor. When he looked up, he saw a circular wall made of blocks of green marble. In the center of the circle was a tubular transport for descending underground.

Luke dreamed that he could see his Jedi Master, Obi-Wan Kenobi, standing at the wall, beckoning him, signaling Luke with a wave of his hand to come closer and enter.

"Luke," said Obi-Wan, "this is the entrance that leads underground to the Lost City of the Jedi. The entire history of the galaxy and all its worlds is recorded there, protected by the caretaker droids of the city. Your destiny is linked to one who lives down there."

Gasping, Luke suddenly awoke from his dream. Beads of sweat dripped from his forehead.

It was early morning. Luke climbed out of bed, walked over to the narrow tower window, and looked down at the treetops of the rain forest. He wondered what his dream meant. Since the day when Obi-Wan Kenobi had been cut down by Darth Vader's lightsaber blade, the Jedi Master had appeared to Luke several times in visions. At the moment of his death, Obi-Wan's body had mysteriously vanished, leaving the physical universe for a world unknown. Obi-Wan Kenobi was a Master of the Force, but now Luke could feel the Force inside himself.

He dressed quickly, walked down the stairs, and climbed into his airspeeder.

Soon he was soaring above the rain forest, just like in his dream, thinking about Obi-Wan Kenobi's mysterious words.

Luke flew the airspeeder faster and faster.

He didn't understand why. He didn't know where he was headed.

He just trusted the Force—and kept going.

What secrets will Luke discover in the Lost City of the Jedi? Who is the "one" who lives there, and how is he linked to Luke's destiny? Find out in *The Lost City of the Jedi*, available now.

Glossary

Admiral Ackbar
Rebel military leader, he is a fishman from the planet Calamari.

Aqualish aliens
Walrus-faced, with smooth skin and large eyes, Aqualish aliens have nasty dispositions. They live on watery planets, and turn their natural aggressions toward all aliens other than their own kind.

Artoo-Detoo (R2-D2)
A barrel-shaped utility droid belonging to Luke Skywalker. Artoo cannot speak in words, but communicates in beeps, buzzes, and whistles that are translated by his companion, See-Threepio (C-3PO). An effective copilot and troubleshooter, Artoo can rapidly penetrate the data system of almost any computer in the galaxy.

Calamarian minisub
A small submarine that Luke, Admiral Ackbar, Threepio, and Artoo use to follow and spy on the huge Whaladon-hunting submarine.

Captain Dunwell
The crazed human captain of the Whaladon-hunting submarine. He wears a blue uniform with medals

and has a neatly trimmed white beard that he likes to tweak.

His great goal is to capture Leviathor, leader of the Whaladons. He has tried to trap Leviathor for many years, throughout the Great War, but every time Leviathor has avoided capture.

Chewbacca
A hairy, eight-foot-tall, 205-year-old Wookiee who serves as copilot aboard the *Millennium Falcon.* Chewbacca (also known as Chewie) uses his strength to assist the Rebel Alliance, usually serving alongside his buddy Han Solo.

Darth Vader
Now deceased, Darth Vader was the second-in-command of the Galactic Empire, serving under the evil Emperor Palpatine. He was born as Annakin Skywalker and was Luke and Leia's father, but he turned to the Dark Side of the Force and tried unsuccessfully to convince Luke to join the Empire. More machine than man, Darth Vader was kept alive by cybernetic devices—and a breathing apparatus built into his black helmet.

Doonium
A heavy metal used by the Empire in most of its war machines.

Domed City of Aquarius
This domed city is located inside a giant bubble under the ocean on the planet Calamari. It was designed for both creatures with lungs and creatures with gills. It has wa-

tery canals with underwater dwellings, and above the canals are markets and homes for air-breathers.

Emdee-Five (MD-5)
An evil Imperial droid with a wide variety of skills, including medical knowledge. MD-5 (called Emdee) is usually at Trioculus's side and always does Trioculus's bidding, no matter what the request. Trioculus has a close relationship with Emdee, much like Luke's relationship with his droids.

Emperor Palpatine
Now deceased, Emperor Palpatine was once a senator in the Old Republic, but he destroyed the old democratic order and established the ruthless Galactic Empire in its place. He ruled the galaxy with military might and tyranny, forcing human and alien citizens of every planet to live in fear. He was assisted by Darth Vader, who eventually turned against him, hurling the Emperor to his death in the power core of the Death Star.

Glove of Darth Vader
The glove of Darth Vader's right hand that was cut off by Luke Skywalker in their final battle.

Grand Moff Dunhausen
A grand moff (high-ranking Imperial governor) who wears earrings shaped like laser pistols, he is lean and very crafty.

Grand Moff Hissa
The grand moff whom Trioculus trusts the most. He has spear-pointed teeth.

Grand Moff Muzzer
A grand moff who is plump and round-faced, he is brash and excitable.

Grand Moff Thistleborn
A grand moff with bushy eyebrows, he is authoritative and very loyal to the Central Committee of Grand Moffs.

Han Solo
A Corellian cargo pilot whose spaceship, the *Millennium Falcon*, served the Rebel Alliance in the fight against the Imperial Death Star. Han is a freewheeling, independent-minded bachelor who usually travels with his Wookiee companion, Chewbacca—but he does have a soft spot for Princess Leia.

Imperial minisub
Attached to the Whaladon-hunting submarine, this is a small probe sub that can seat four or five people. It also serves as an escape sub in the event of an emergency.

Leviathor
The leader of the Whaladons, he is the ancient one who knows the entire history of his species. He is a wise and great ruler, and his leadership has helped many Whaladons to remain free by outsmarting the Whaladon hunters.

Leviathor is a white Whaladon—the only great white still alive.

Luke Skywalker
A Jedi Knight from Tatooine, now a Commander in the Rebel Alliance. Luke was trained in the secret knowledge

of the Force by Obi-Wan Kenobi and Yoda. Princess Leia is his twin sister.

Mon Mothma
A distinguished-looking leader, she has long been in charge of the Rebel Alliance.

Obi-Wan Kenobi
Obi-Wan Kenobi was a Jedi Master who taught Luke Skywalker to use the Force. Obi-Wan passed away when he was defeated by Darth Vader in a lightsaber duel, but he is still sometimes seen by Luke in dreams and visions.

Phobium
A metal that Emperor Palpatine used to coat the power core of the Death Star.

Princess Leia Organa
Raised by a senator of the Old Republic on Alderaan, a planet that was destroyed by the Empire, Princess Leia is Luke Skywalker's twin sister. Courageous and outspoken, she is a valuable member of the Rebel Alliance in its fight against Imperial forces.

See-Threepio (C-3PO)
A golden, human-shaped protocol droid belonging to Luke Skywalker, See-Threepio can translate six million galactic languages and is an expert at droid-human relations. He is seldom seen without his sidekick, Artoo-Detoo (R2-D2).

Trioculus (pronounced *Try-ock-you-luss*)
Supreme Slavelord of the spice mines of the planet Kessel.
After the death of Emperor Palpatine, he comes forward
announcing that he is the Emperor's banished son. He is
a handsome but evil mutant with three eyes, including an
evil eye on his forehead that has hypnotic powers.

Valley of the Giant Oysters
An undersea valley on the planet Calamari that has been
the home of the giant oysters for millions of years.

Whaladons
Whale-like mammals that live underwater on Calamari,
the water world that is the home of the respected Rebel,
Admiral Ackbar, a fishman. Led by the white Whaladon
Leviathor, Whaladons resemble humpback whales but
have a few variations.

Whaladon hunters
Walrus-faced Aqualish aliens who serve under Captain
Dunwell on the Whaladon-hunting submarine.

Whaladon-hunting submarine
This terrifying vessel is as big as an Imperial space battle
cruiser or a small city. Its job is to stun Whaladons and
then suck them into the many on-board storage chambers.
This submarine can store more than a dozen Whaladons
at one time.

Whaladon Processing Center
This is a bleak Imperial installation inside an undersea
crater. Here the bodies of Whaladons are stripped of their

meat and blubber, then loaded into Imperial cargo spaceships to be shipped to places where it is needed.

Yoda
The Jedi Master Yoda was a small creature who lived on
the bog planet Dagobah. For eight hundred years before
passing away he taught Jedi Knights, including Obi-Wan
Kenobi and Luke Skywalker.

About the Authors

PAUL DAVIDS and **HOLLACE DAVIDS** met by chance in Harvard Square in 1971, just after Paul saw George Lucas's first movie, *THX-1138*. It was love at first sight. Paul had graduated from Princeton and Hollace from Goucher and from the master's program in counseling at Boston University. But they discovered that they had grown up just a few miles apart in Bethesda and Silver Spring, Maryland. They married several months after they first met.

Paul, who began making 8mm science fiction movies when he was ten, studied writing and directing at the American Film Institute in L.A., and a few years later became a member of the Writers Guild (WGA), writing for Cornel Wilde and (with Hollace) George Pal, a pioneer of movie science fiction. After teaching children with learning disabilities, Hollace became the FILMEX Society Coordinator for the L.A. International Film Exposition.

In 1977, the year *Star Wars* premiered, their daughter Jordan was born. In 1980, the year *The Empire Strikes Back* opened, their son Scott was born, and Hollace began coordinating all the major film premieres and parties for Columbia Pictures. And when *Return of the Jedi* opened in 1983, Paul's accomplishments included writing *She Dances Alone*, a movie starring Bud Cort and Max von Sydow, and producing for the TV show *Lie Detector*. He then worked as production coordinator for about one hundred episodes of *The Transformers*, some of which he wrote. Currently Paul is an executive producer of a movie for HBO based on the book *UFO Crash at Roswell*, and Hollace is vice president of publicity and special events for TriStar Pictures.

Paul and Hollace published their first book in 1986, *The Fires of Pele*, a fantasy about Mark Twain in Hawaii. Now they are hard at work on even more Star Wars books for young readers.

About the Illustrators

BENTON JEW began working for Industrial Light & Magic in 1988, even before his graduation from the Academy of Art College and the University of San Francisco. After receiving his B.F.A. in illustration, he continued to work in the art department, contributing numerous concept designs and storyboard artwork for feature films, commercials, and theme-park attractions. His storyboard art for film includes *Ghostbusters 2*, *The Doors*, *Memoirs of an Invisible Man*, and *The Hunt for Red October*. His commercials include Reebok, Merrill Lynch, M&M Mars, Burger King, and Heinz. Mr. Jew lives and works in San Rafael, California.

KARL KESEL was born in 1959 and raised in the small town of Victor, New York. He started reading comic books at the age of ten, while traveling cross-country with his family, and decided soon after he wanted to become a cartoonist. By the age of twenty-five, he landed a full-time job as an illustrator for DC Comics, working on such titles as *Superman*, *World's Finest*, *Newsboy Legion*, and *Hawk and Dove*, which he also cowrote. He was also one of the artists on *The Terminator* and *Indiana Jones* miniseries for Dark Horse

Comics. Mr. Kesel lives and works with his wife, Barbara, in Milwaukie, Oregon.

DREW STRUZAN is a teacher, lecturer, and one of the most influential forces working in commercial art today. His strong visual sense and recognizable style have produced lasting pieces of art for advertising, the recording industry, and motion pictures. His paintings include the album covers for *Alice Cooper's Greatest Hits* and *Welcome to My Nightmare*, which was recently voted one of the one hundred classic album covers of all time by *Rolling Stone* magazine. He has also created the movie posters for Star Wars, *E.T. The Extra-Terrestrial*, the Back to the Future series, the Indiana Jones series, *An American Tale*, and *Hook*. Mr. Struzan lives and works in the California valley with his wife Cheryle. Their son, Christian, is continuing in the family tradition, working as an art director and illustrator.

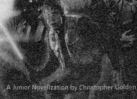